Maya Was
Grumpy

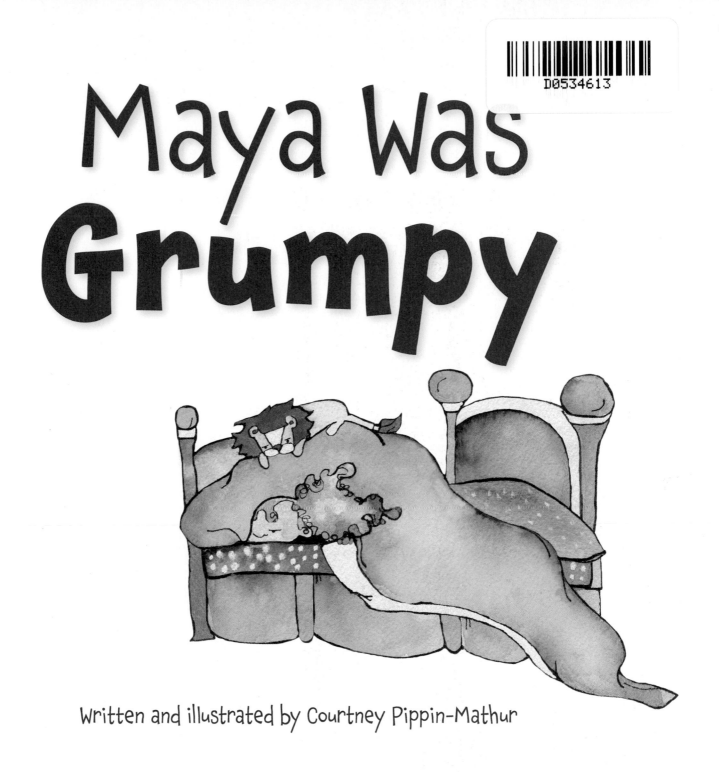

Written and illustrated by Courtney Pippin-Mathur

SCHOLASTIC INC.

To Saurabh Mathur for always believing in me,
and to Kiran who is never, ever grumpy. -CPM

ISBN 978-0-545-62077-2

12 11 10 9 8 7 6 5 4   15 16 17 18/0

Printed in the U.S.A.   40

First Scholastic printing, September 2013

Editor: Shari Dash Greenspan
Graphic Design: The Virtual Paintbrush
This book was typeset in Chaloops.
The illustrations were rendered in pencil, ink,
and watercolor, with a little digital magic.

Maya was **grumpy**.

She didn't know **why** she was grumpy.
She was just in a
crispy, cranky,
grumpy,
grouchy
mood.

She didn't want to read
or color or eat banana chips,

or wear her favorite shorts, or go outside and play.

The only thing Maya wanted to do
was **grouch** around the house and share her **bad mood**.

She **grumped** into Gramma's room and **snarled** at the cat.

He just stretched and went back to sleep.

She **glumped** into the living room and made faces at some birds.

They just flew away.

She **clumped** into the kitchen and
grumbled at her brothers.

They just glopped their food around.

Finally, Maya **thumped** up
behind Gramma and **growled**
as loudly as she could.

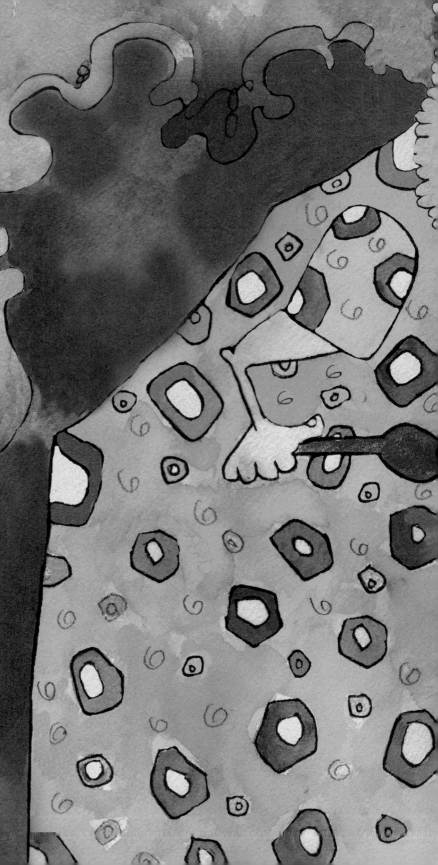

"Feeling a bit **grumpy** today?" Gramma asked.

Maya just **scowled**.

"Well then," said Gramma, "I guess that means no hunting for hippos after breakfast."

"I never hunt for hippos,"
Maya **grouched**.

"And no putting your head
in a crocodile's mouth
before lunch."

"That's just silly,"
Maya **grumbled**.

"Bathing baby elephants would probably be a bad idea today if you're grumpy," Gramma said.

Maya **rolled** her eyes.

"Certainly no tickling tarantulas until they giggle," Gramma added.

Maya shook her head.
A **tingle** in her belly
tickled all the way up
to her mouth, but she
squeezed her lips
into a tight line.

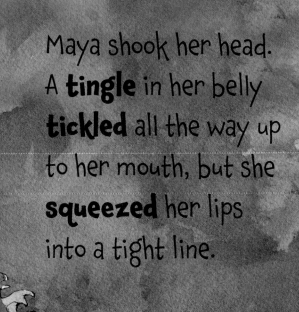

"I did have plans to slide down the neck of a giraffe later," Gramma explained, "but I guess we can reschedule."

Maya felt a **wiggle** reach
the corners of her frown.

"And definitely no swinging
with monkeys today
if you're grumpy."

A bubbly **giggle** escaped through Maya's lips. "Swinging with monkeys might be nice," she said...

...and she gave Gramma a big **hug**.

Gramma packed a snack and fixed Maya's hair.

Then they all went outside to find
the hippos,
crocodiles,
elephants,
tarantulas,
giraffes,
and monkeys...

...and Maya felt **much** better.